Crocodiles are the Best Animals of All copyright © Frances Lincoln Limited 2009
Text copyright © Sean Taylor 2009
Illustrations copyright © Hannah Shaw 2009
The right of Sean Taylor and Hannah Shaw to be identified respectively as the author
and illustrator of this work has been asserted by them in accordance with the Copyright,
Designs and Patents Act, 1988 (United Kingdom).

First published in Great Britain and in the USA in 2009 by
Frances Lincoln Children's Books, 4 Torriano Mews,
Torriano Avenue, London NW5 2RZ
www.franceslincoln.com

A catalogue record for this book is available from the British Library.

ISBN 978-1-84507-904-8

Illustrated with pen and ink and scanned textures
Typeset in Later On

Printed in Dongguan, Guangdong, China
by TOPPAN Leefung in October 2009

3 5 7 9 8 6 4 2

CROCODILES ARE THE BEST ANIMALS OF ALL!

by SEAN TAYLOR

illustrated by HANNAH SHAW

F
FRANCES LINCOLN
CHILDREN'S BOOKS

A donkey gave a nod of his head.

He chewed a bit and then he said,

"My ears may wiggle and my teeth may be wonky,

but nothing is better than being a donkey!"

"I AM BETTER!" came a loud boast. "I could eat you for breakfast with buttered toast!"

Up came a crocodile, swimming front crawl.

He said, "**CROCODILES ARE THE BEST ANIMALS OF ALL!**"

He did it without a slip or a fall,

hissing,

"CROCODILES ARE THE BEST ANIMALS OF ALL!"

"I nibble grass and seedlings and shoots!
I even chomp up Wellington boots!"

He nibbled towards them with a growl and a call,

"CROCODILES ARE THE BEST ANIMALS OF ALL!"

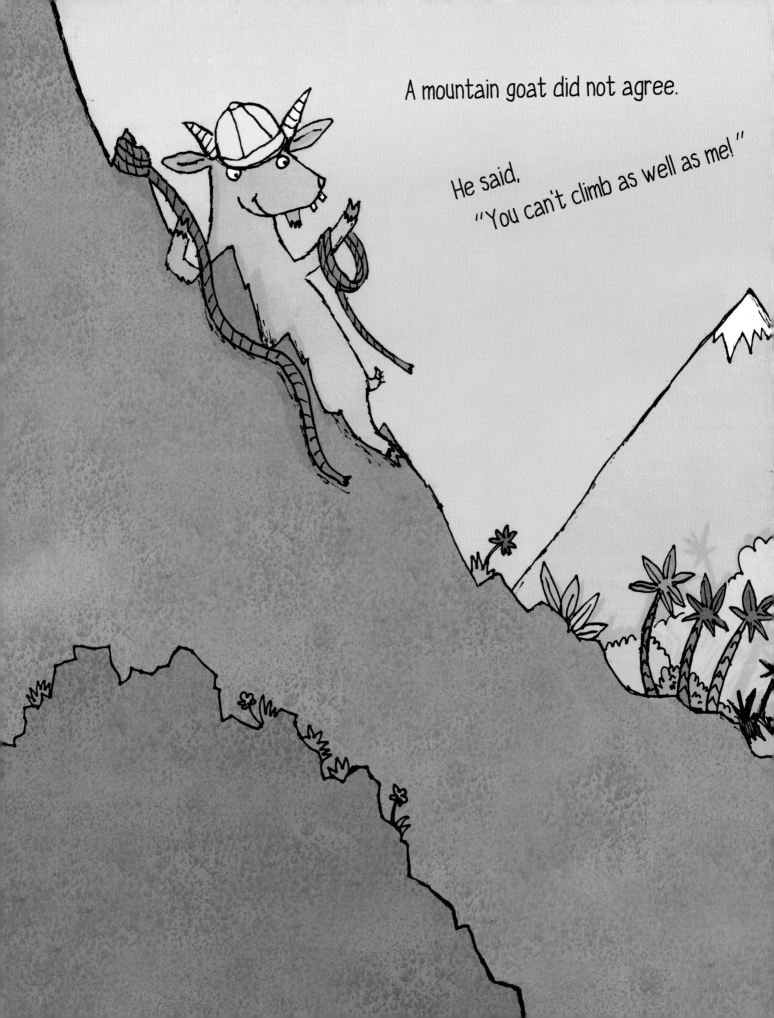

A mountain goat did not agree.

He said,
"You can't climb as well as me!"

"Pish Posh!" said the crocodile. "I can climb
And play the bongos at the same time!"

He clambered a mountain until he looked very small,

shouting, "**CROCODILES ARE THE BEST ANIMALS OF ALL!**"

He bounced about like a basket ball,
chuckling,

"CROCODILES ARE THE BEST ANIMALS OF ALL!"

The crocodile grinned. He had won the day.

But then he heard the donkey say,

"You're good at many things, I can see,

but you cannot wiggle your ears like me."

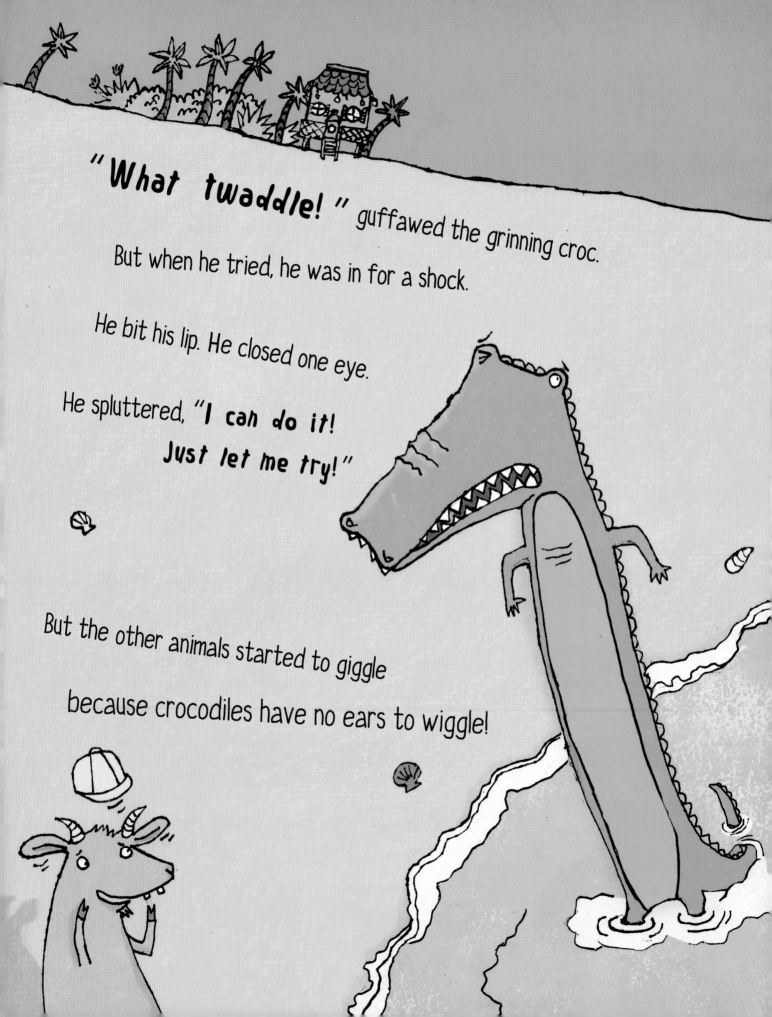

"**What twaddle!**" guffawed the grinning croc.

But when he tried, he was in for a shock.

He bit his lip. He closed one eye.

He spluttered, "**I can do it!
Just let me try!**"

But the other animals started to giggle

because crocodiles have no ears to wiggle!

The donkey gave a nod of his head.

He chewed a bit and then he said,

"My ears may wiggle and my teeth may be wonky,

but **nothing is better** than being a donkey!"